Tomek Bogacki

Cat and Mouse
in the Night

Frances Foster Books
Farrar Straus Giroux

NEW YORK

Early one morning, three little mice left their home, as they did every day.

To Frances

Copyright © 1998 by Tomek Bogacki

All rights reserved

Distributed in Canada by Douglas & McIntyre Ltd.

Printed and bound in the United States of America

Designed by Monika Keano

First edition, 1998

Library of Congress Cataloging-in-Publication Data

Bogacki, Tomasz.

Cat and mouse in the night / Tomek Bogacki. — 1st ed.

p. cm.

"Frances Foster books."

Summary: Their inattentiveness strands a little mouse and a little cat in the meadow after dark, where their fear turns into a wonderful discovery.

ISBN 0-374-31190-0

[1. Mice—Fiction. 2. Cats—Fiction. 3. Night—Fiction.]

I. Title.

PZ7.B6357825Can   1998   97-30160

[E]—dc21

And three little cats left their home, too.

They met in the meadow and played together all day long, until the sun went down.

"It's getting late. It's time to go home,"
said the little mice.

"It's getting dark. We should go home, too,"
said the little cats.

But one little mouse and one little cat did
not pay attention to the others.

They kept on playing. Suddenly the world around them looked very different.

"It's so dark here," said the frightened
little cat.
"We shouldn't have stayed out so late," said
the little mouse in a trembling voice.

They heard a strange sound above
their heads.
"Who-hoo-hoo!"

"Don't be afraid," said the owl. "It's a beautiful night."

"A beautiful night?" wondered the little mouse and the little cat. "It's so dark and scary."

"Oh, you must see it from the top of the tree," said the owl.

Then the little cat and the little mouse became curious, so they followed the owl up, up, up to the top of the tree.

"Look!" said the owl.
The moon shone and the stars sparkled.
"Oh!" said the cat and the mouse. "It is beautiful!"

Next morning, the other little cats and the
other little mice went out to look for their
brother and their sister.
"Why didn't you come home last night?"
asked the little mice.

"Where were you?" asked the little cats.
"Wait and we will show you," answered their
brother and sister, mysteriously.

At the end of the day, when it began to get dark, the little cat and the little mouse showed their brothers and sisters how to climb the big tree.

"Look!" they said when they reached the top.
"Oh!" said the others in amazement.
And they all spent the night at the top of the
tree, close to the moon and the stars, just
watching.